**KLaSKY CSUPO** INC.

Based on the TV series *Rugrats*® created by Klasky/Csupo Inc. and Paul Germain as seen on Nickelodeon®

SIMON SPOTLIGHT
An imprint of Simon & Schuster Children's Publishing Division
1230 Avenue of the Americas
New York, New York 10020

Manufactured in the United States of America

First Edition      10 9 8 7 6 5 4 3 2 1

ISBN 0-689-81678-2

Library of Congress Catalog Card Number 98-60084

## Acknowledgments

I'd like to say a few words of thanks to the many people who helped make this book a reality.

First of all, my son Sam would like to point out that I never could have written this book without him. "If I hadn't been watching *Rugrats*, you wouldn't have known about the show." He's right.

Another round of thanks to Paula Kaplan, Heather Morgan, and Louise Gikow for their contributions, along with the members of Sam's focus group—Katie Dunitz and Josh Tichauer—who taught me which words didn't belong in a book that could be read by children. Thanks to Mike Ansell for lending me his lights, my editors at Simon & Schuster and Nickelodeon Books, Mel Berger and Claudia Cross at William Morris, and finally, everybody at Klasky Csupo Inc. for opening their doors to me and showing me how cartoons are made.

**Chuckie:** Tommy, aren't you sleepy?

**Tommy:** No . . . I'm thinkin'.

**Chuckie:** 'Bout what?

**Tommy:** Robots.

**Chuckie:** Don't think about that, Tommy. You'll get bad dreams.

**Tommy:** I can't help it because, well . . . maybe anybody could be robots.

**Chuckie:** Like who?

**Tommy:** Like anybody, Chuckie, like the mailman or the man who sells ice cream or . . . EVEN OUR OWN MOMS AND DADS.

**Angelica:** "That's a really dumb question that only a baby-bottle sucker would ask."

Rugrats rule! Since it was first broadcast on Nickelodeon back in 1991, *Rugrats* has become the number one entertainment show on cable TV. The world's "bestest" babies—Tommy, Chuckie, Phil and Lil, Angelica, and their pals—are all over books, dolls, toys, clothing, and lots of other merchandise. And they now have their own feature-length movie.

How did *Rugrats* get so big? How did it begin? What goes into making the show? Who are the people who lend their voices to the characters? Stay tuned for the answers to all these questions and more. There's also a complete list and description of every *Rugrats* cartoon at the end of this book.

# The Rugrats

## NEIGHBORHOOD

**Tommy Pickles:** One-year-old leader of the babies

**Stu Pickles:** Tommy's toy-inventor dad

**Didi Pickles:** Tommy's mom, a teacher

**Grandpa Lou Pickles:** Tommy's fun-loving grandfather (Stu's dad)

**Grandpa Boris:** Didi's dad

**Grandma Minka:** Didi's mom

**Spike:** Tommy's dog

**Angelica Pickles:** Tommy's three-year-old bully cousin

**Drew Pickles:** Angelica's dad (Stu's brother)

**Charlotte Pickles:** Angelica's working mom (Tommy's aunt)

**Chuckie Finster:** Tommy's best friend and next-door neighbor

**Charles (Chaz) Finster Sr.:** Chuckie's dad

**Phil and Lil DeVille:** Tommy's identical twin pals. They live next door to Tommy on the other side.

**Betty DeVille:** Didi's best friend and Phil and Lil's mom

**Howard DeVille:** Phil and Lil's dad

**Susie Carmichaels:** Tommy's three-year-old neighbor

# Chapter One

## THE HiSTORY OF THE RUGRATS

"You guys, I don't think this is a good idea."

–Chuckie Finster

On busy Highland Avenue in Hollywood, California, large paintings of Tommy, Chuckie, Angelica, and the rest of the Rugrats gang decorate the side of a building. This is where *Rugrats* was created and where the cartoons are made.

Inside the building are Tommy's *real* mom and dad. Their names are Arlene Klasky and Gabor Csupo (pronounced CHOOP-oh), and they own the cartoon factory called Klasky Csupo. Here more than two hundred artists draw pictures, writers dream up stories, and actors record the voices for *Rugrats* and other 'toons.

The odd shapes and unusual colors and designs of Klasky Csupo 'toons set them apart from many others, and many people say that's because of Gabor Csupo's past. He grew up in Hungary, where he attended art school and studied animation at Hungary's famous Pannonia studio. He wanted to have his own art studio and draw his own creations, but under Hungary's Communist government, people were not always free to start their own businesses. So, in 1975, Gabor decided to leave Hungary. Special permission was required to leave—and this was almost impossible to get. Gabor took his chances and snuck out of the country. He took a really scary two-and-a-half-hour-long walk through a darkened railway tunnel to Austria. A friend was waiting for him, and he helped Gabor get a job in Sweden as an artist. There he met his future wife, Arlene Klasky, who was also an artist. They fell in love and moved to Los Angeles. (Gabor and Arlene have since divorced.)

Gabor worked at the famous Hanna-Barbera cartoon studio on their *Scooby Doo* TV show. Arlene worked for advertising agencies, the companies that make TV, newspaper, and magazine ads. In 1982 Gabor and Arlene decided to work together and follow through on Gabor's dream of having his own studio. They called it Klasky Csupo and began by designing the artwork you see at the beginning of TV shows—called logos. They also did the animation—the process of making cartoons—for TV commercials.

Klasky Csupo's first big animation hit began as one-minute shorts that ran on *The Tracey Ullman Show.* Bart, Lisa, Marge, Homer, and Maggie Simpson were first seen on this show, and these cartoons soon grew into a huge sensation. The cartoon family got their own show, *The Simpsons.* Klasky Csupo animated the first three years of the series, from 1989 to 1992, and the show became wildly popular. In fact, back then it was

Gabor Csupo

Arlene Klasky

Klasky Csupo Studio

pretty hard to walk down the street and not see someone wearing a Bart Simpson "Eat My Shorts" T-shirt.

It's hard to imagine, but there was once a time when the Simpsons weren't yellow. At first, *The Simpsons* creator Matt Groening handed Gabor Csupo his black-and-white drawings, and Gabor made the big color decisions. It was Csupo who decided to give the Simpson family yellow skin and blue hair for Marge. "Everybody kept saying, 'You're crazy, nobody has yellow skin and blue hair!'" recalls Csupo. "And we said, 'Why not?'"

The success of *The Simpsons* rubbed off on everyone associated with it. In 1990, a few months after it premiered, Nickelodeon asked Klasky Csupo to suggest some original 'toon ideas.

Arlene Klasky didn't have to look any farther than her kids' room.

"My second child, Brandon, was fifteen months old at the time," she recalls. "Staying at home with my kids, I thought it was interesting to watch my children and see what motivated them, because what they were interested in was a lot different from adults. To them, getting to the bathroom or opening doors was a big deal."

Paul Germain, a TV writer who produced *The Simpsons* shorts for Klasky Csupo, was hired by Arlene and Gabor to help create new shows for them. Arlene called Germain one night with an idea she had for a show about a baby's view of life—*Rugrats.* He added

Paul Germain

the concept that the babies could talk—but only to one another.

"The thing about babies," says Paul Germain, "is that you look at them and think they don't know anything. But as adults we learn that babies are a lot

> **Tommy:** "We're supposed to get in trouble. That's our job."

smarter than we think. And that's how it is for kids in general. They know a lot more than we think. And that's what the series is all about."

The first character created was Tommy, who was named after Germain's son. He's equally inspired by Gabor and Arlene's son, Brandon Csupo, since Gabor drew Tommy Pickles to look like young Brandon—pigeon-toed, skinny legs, big head, and almost no hair.

Klasky Csupo's Peter Chung drew Angelica and Spike, the dog, while Arlene Klasky drew Phil and Lil and grandparents Boris and Minka, based on her Russian relatives. Gabor drew everyone else.

Rugrats co-creator Gabor Csupo with sons Brandon (in his arms) and Jarrett. Tommy was drawn to look like Brandon. Notice his pigeon toes?

Arlene's Russian relatives. She drew Grandpa Boris and Grandma Minka to look like them.

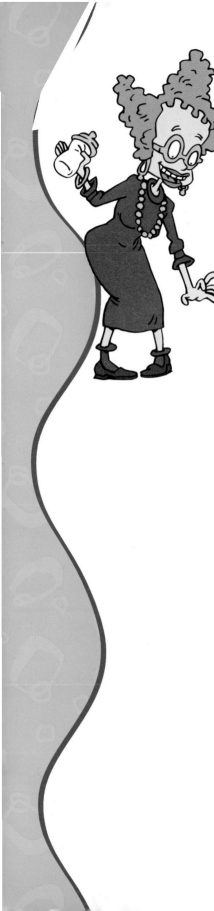

Arlene Klasky is a lot like Didi.

"When I was a first-time parent, I had no idea how to raise a baby, and I kept turning to these childhood instructional books," she says. "That's where I learned how to take care of children. I didn't trust myself at first."

And Gabor Csupo resembles Stu. Like Tommy's toy-inventor dad, he is a very creative person.

The show was named after the term "rugrats," meaning little kids who crawl around on a rug most of the time.

One-year-old Tommy was created to be the hero of the show. He leads all the adventures, while his friend Chuckie is the guy who's always scared about what kind of trouble they'll get into. Tommy's friends Phil and Lil often join them on their adventures, and all four are always against Tommy's bossy three-year-old cousin Angelica. The writers later added another kid—three-year-old Susie—as a nice alternative to Angelica.

When Klasky Csupo went back to Nickelodeon with a more detailed outline for the show, they were given the go-ahead to make a sample *Rugrats* cartoon, called a pilot. Producers begin with a pilot to show what the program will be like. If the network likes it, they give the producers the go-ahead to start making weekly episodes.

Klasky Csupo produced a six-and-a-half-minute *Rugrats* pilot in 1990. It was about Tommy thinking the potty was alive. Based on that short cartoon, Nickelodeon told Klasky Csupo to make thirteen episodes of *Rugrats.*

One of the big questions people always ask is: Where's Chuckie's mom? Here's what happened. Since all the other babies have two parents, the *Rugrats* producers thought it would be more interesting to let Chuckie's dad be a single parent. They also thought it would be cute if Chuckie looked and acted just like Charles Finster Sr.

But they couldn't make up their minds about why Charles Sr. was single. Either alternative—that Chuckie's mom had died or that his parents were divorced—seemed so sad. The writers and producers spent many years discussing Chuckie's mom, but couldn't come up with a decision until 1997, when we learned that Chuckie's mom had died soon after he was born.

Why did Klasky Csupo wait so long to tell people about Chuckie's mom? "Death is a very tragic subject and it's not something we wanted to deal with in the early years of the series," says Gabor Csupo. "The audience hardly knew the characters then. But people were always wondering about Chuckie's mom, so we thought the time was finally right to explain what happened to her."

Once Klasky Csupo got *Rugrats* on Nickelodeon, they started getting a reputation for unique, original cartoons. They went on to make Nickelodeon's *Aaahh!!! Real Monsters* and the USA Network's *Duckman* and *Santo Bugito*, which aired on CBS in 1995–96. They also did some of the ABC *Edith Ann* specials.

Big eyes (Tommy and the Real Monsters), stick figures with features on the side (Duckman, Oblina), and of course, a yellow family are just some of the Klasky Csupo trademarks, along with eye-popping colors not usually seen on television.

Inside of Klasky Csupo Studios

One of the reasons their cartoons look so different may be that, like Gabor, so many of the artists are from Eastern Europe and Russia, and their styles of drawing haven't been seen on TV in the United States in the past. In fact, inside the studio is a large map on the bulletin board that indicates the homes of Klasky Csupo's nearly two hundred-person staff, and the largest cluster of pins in the map are in Europe.

Here's Gabor Csupo on animation: "When we started, we had this goal never to imitate the styles out there. We thought there was a place for a new generation of cartoons.

"Everybody was just imitating the already successful formulas of Disney and Warner Brothers. Everybody was just drawing the same kind of characters with a little bit of a different haircut and a different outfit, but nothing was new. We just felt that the new generation of kids was ready for something else besides the big-nosed, big rounded shiny-eyed characters they'd seen in the last fifty years.

"I thought a different type of new design would probably get more attention than if we just tried to imitate the ones on every TV channel."

The look had a lot to do with the success of *Rugrats*, but perhaps the most important thing was the theme of the show, which fits nicely with what Nickelodeon is all about: That even at a very young age, kids can take care of their problems and be self-sufficient, if they just put their minds to it.

*Rugrats* was one of three Nicktoons that first aired on Nickelodeon on Sunday, August 11, 1991. The others were *Doug* and *The Ren and Stimpy Show.*

All of them did well, although it was the wacky, weird humor of *Ren and Stimpy* that received the most attention at first.

**Angelica:** "You babies think you're so big! Ha! You're not big. You're just big babies!"

In fact, *Rugrats* really didn't take off in a big way until early 1995, after Nickelodeon had stopped making new *Rugrats* shows. The first sixty-five episodes had been completed, and Nick felt they had enough. But when Nick started playing *Rugrats* reruns Monday through Friday, the show began to catch on. Kids started talking about the show and telling their friends. Adults started watching too.

**Chuckie:** "What are we gonna do, Tommy, what are we gonna do?"

The *Rugrats'* TV ratings started to climb. (Ratings are polls that ask people what shows they like to watch on TV.) *Rugrats* turned into not just the number one show on Nickelodeon, but the number one entertainment program on cable TV as well.

An average 18.6 million kids watch *Rugrats* every week. And the show has won three Emmy awards, TV's highest honor, two for Outstanding Children's Animated Program and one for Outstanding Achievement in Animation.

Even though Nickelodeon originally thought they had enough *Rugrats* cartoons to last a lifetime, the show became so huge that they had to change their plan. In 1996, production began on twenty-six new episodes of the show, to be aired throughout 1997, along with a full-length *Rugrats* movie, released in late 1998.

## MEET THE RUGRATS

Tommy Pickles

**Role:** The leader of the Rugrats

**Character:** Tommy is the one-year-old son of Stu and Didi Pickles. To him, the world is one gigantic playground.

**Best known for:** Crawling around in his diapers and leading adventures

**Personality:** Tommy wants to explore everything, no matter what happens.

**Usually seen wearing:** A blue shirt and diapers

**Line:** "A baby's gotta do what a baby's gotta do."

**His feet are:** Pigeon-toed

**He has led imaginary adventures to:** The North Pole, the jungle, inside Chuckie, Mirrorland, and the Wild West

**An expert at:** Breaking out of the crib

**Favorite tool:** Tommy's plastic toy screwdriver always comes in handy when breaking out of the crib.

**The first movie he ever saw:** *The Dummi Bears*

**Favorite character:** Reptar, the dinosaur monster, featured in movies and on Reptar cereal boxes and candy bars (which turn your tongue green after eating them), is Tommy's favorite character.

**Favorite ice-cream flavor:** Chocolate swirl

**Scared of:** Monsters and robots

**To Tommy, the funniest thing in the world is:** When milk comes out of your nose

**Calls the light inside the refrigerator:** Mr. Light

### A Tommy moment:

"Remember that big crash in the garage that Chuckie and me toldja about? Well, I saw Spike in the kitchen when it happened. He couldna done it! Someone—or something—is making trouble, and it's not Spike!"

Tommy is played by:

**E. G. Daily**

E. G. Daily's other cartoon voices include: Mambo on Klasky Csupo's *Duckman* and roles on *Eek the Cat, Duck Daze,* and *Problem Child.* She has appeared in more than fifteen films, including *Pee Wee's Big Adventure*, *Valley Girl,* and *Streets of Fire*. And what does E. G. stand for? All she'll say is, "Extra Little Girlie."

**Role:** Tommy's sidekick

**Character:** Chuckie is Tommy's two-year-old best friend and next-door neighbor.

**Personality:** 'Fraidy-cat. Tends to be scared of Tommy's schemes. Complains a lot, but has a very colorful imagination.

**Best known for his:** Large mop of red hair and big glasses and three freckles on each cheek

**Often wears:** A blue shirt with a picture of Saturn, and green shorts

**Line:** "You guys, I don't think this is such a good idea."

**Likes:** Tommy, because he isn't afraid of anything

**Chuckie's scariest moment:** When his head got stuck in a sock

**Adventure highlights:** Learning how to use the potty, becoming a superhero, and freeing his pet sea monkeys at the beach

**It was Chuckie's idea that:** On the other side of mirrors is a reverse world called Mirrorland.

**Chuckie once believed:** The sky was falling and the end of the world was near. He was also led to believe he was turning into a Rhinoceros due to the Angelica-created disease "Rhinoceritis."

## A Chuckie moment:

**Tommy:** You know what we gotta do now, don't you Chuckie?

**Chuckie:** Yeah. We gotta find somethin' else to play with.

**Tommy:** No, we gotta go down there and get my plane.

**Chuckie:** Tommy, we can't do that. We're babies. We don't know how to go down stairs.

**Tommy:** Well, we gotta learn sometime.

**Chuckie:** Yeah, that's true . . . maybe next year.

Chuckie is played by:

**Christine Cavanaugh**

She also does the voice of Oblina on *Aaahh!!! Real Monsters*. But besides monsters and babies, her other big role was that of a pig. Cavanaugh did the voice of Babe the pig in the 1994 movie *Babe*. Other voices include roles on the cartoons *Darkwing Duck*, *Sonic the Hedgehog*, *Dexter's Lab*, *Sing Me a Story*, and *Cathy*.

**Role:** Bully

**Character:** Tommy's three-year-old cousin

**Personality:** The boss. She acts sweet when she's near adults, but when they turn their backs . . .

**Often wears:** A purple jumper and an orange, striped blouse. And she wears her hair in pigtails.

**Line:** "If I wanna be mean, I can be mean. Know why? 'Cause I'm the boss!"

**She says:** She's the cutest girl ever born, the best singer, and the most talented dancer. The truth: No, she isn't.

**Calls Tommy:** "Melonhead"

**If something bad happens:** Angelica insists she didn't do it.

**Special talent:** Can talk in such a way that both adults and babies can understand

**Likes to play with:** Her doll Cynthia

**Loves:** Sweets. Angelica will do almost anything to get her hands on cookies or candy.

**Once sued her parents because:** They asked her to eat broccoli . . . but it was all really a dream.

### An Angelica moment:

**Tommy:** Gimme my ball!

**Angelica:** Say pretty please with sugar on top.

**Tommy:** Gimme my ball.

**Angelica:** Say Angelica is the nicest, prettiest, bestest person in the whole wide world.

**Tommy:** Gimme my BALL!

**Angelica:** Well, if you can't be nicer than that, I guess you'll never see your dumb old ball again.

Angelica is played by:

**Cheryl Chase**

Besides Angelica, she did several voices on the first two seasons of *The Ren and Stimpy Show*, the *Betty Boop* cartoon, the sound effects for Pubert Addams in the movie *Addams Family Values*, and the voice of May in the movie *My Neighbor Totoro.*

## Phil and Lil DeVille

**Role:** To comment on the antics of Tommy, Chuckie, and Angelica

**Characters:** The fifteen-month-old twins who live on the other side of the Pickleses' house. They do everything together.

**Personality:** They always go along with Tommy's plans and act as his soldiers.

**Their mom says:** "You couldn't find two kids in the whole world who love each other more than my little pumpkins."

**Often wear:** Green overalls and blue shoes (Phil) and a green jumper and pink shoes (Lil). Lil also wears a pink bow in her hair—and Phil doesn't.

**Once starred in:** A TV commercial for diapers

**They like:** Completing each other's sentences, blaming each other for stuff, and gross things

**They dislike:** Being mistaken for one another—especially by their parents

**A great present from Phil and Lil:** A box of worms or mud

**What Phil calls Chuckie's freckles:** "Freckers"

### A Phil and Lil moment (on what a toilet might be):

**Phil:** Is that the thing I saw our dog drinking out of? I thought it was a big water dish.

**Lil:** I think it's a fishbowl.

**Phil:** A fishbowl? There's no fish in that thing, Lillian.

**Lil:** Well, I saw something swimming around in there, Philip.

Phil and Lil are played by:
**Kath Soucie**
She also does Betty DeVille, and was Lola Bunny in *Space Jam* and Casper on Fox's *Casper, the Friendly Ghost* cartoon.

**Role:** Tommy's busy and absentminded dad

**Character:** Runs his own toy manufacturing company, Pickles Industries, out of his workshop in the basement

**Personality:** Always dresses sloppily and competes with his successful businessman brother Drew

**Often wears:** Messy clothes. And he usually has stubble on his face because he forgot to shave.

**Line:** "Didi, I make toys for a living. I can slap this together in no time."

**Toy inventions include:** Patty Pants dolls; the Mr. Friend robot toy; the Stu Pickles Automatic Sofa, a remote control-operated sofa that vibrates; and the Wacko Specs, toy glasses with exploding eyes

**Often:** Bursts out of the basement with a new toy for Tommy to try out or a kitchen gadget for wife Didi to experiment with

**Famous last words:** "This is the toy that's going to put Pickle Industries on the map!"

**Once:** Forgot who he was and thought he was a baby

**Like his wife:** Stu has no idea his son can talk when he's not around.

**Sometimes calls Tommy:** Champ

---

## A Stu moment (on how to use a calculator):

**Stu:** You activate the fractal cursor here, then perambulate your actual sum times this thing, which is the vector factor, and correlate the decimal point minus the cost of your groceries. Get it?

**Grandpa:** Nope.

**Stu:** Don't worry, Pop. You'll figure it out.

---

Stu is played by:
**Jack Riley**
A well-known actor seen on Nick-at-Nite's *Bob Newhart Show* as Mr. Carlin, Riley has also appeared on many radio commercials. Stu is his only cartoon voice.

**Role:** Overprotective mother

**Character:** Stu's wife and Tommy's mom. A teacher, she can often be found reading every book ever written on how to raise children.

**Personality:** Worried that she's not a good mom

**Line:** "They are a handful sometimes, but they are so adorable."

**Her hair:** Looks like a mountain of orange-raspberry sorbet

**So worried about Tommy that:** she rarely even notices when he takes off on one of his adventures

**Her idol:** Child-care expert Dr. Lipschitz

**Likes:** Junk shops and garage sales

## A Didi moment:

**Didi:** Well, according to the Lipschitz baby book, as soon as the first teeth appear, it's time to take the baby to . . . you know where.

**Stu:** I just can't believe you want to take him to the dentist.

**Didi:** Don't say "dentist." You'll scare him. Just say "tooth fairy." It sounds nicer.

Didi is played by:

**Melanie Chartoff**

She also does the voice of Didi's mother Minka, and Nora on the cartoon version of *Jumanji.* As an actress, she played the principal on Fox's *Parker Lewis Can't Lose,* and appeared on ABC's *Fridays* comedy series.

## Grandpa Lou Pickles

**Role:** Baby-sitter

**Character:** Stu's dad and Tommy's grandfather. Lives upstairs in the Pickleses' house, and often baby-sits for Tommy and the other Rugrats.

**Personality:** Easygoing and absentminded; always on the babies' side if disagreement exists

**Line:** "Oh, for the love of Betsy, it's only a mouse! Why, in my day, we thought nothing of finding herds of elk living in our garage."

**Tommy, on his best pal:** "Who takes care of me when I'm sick? GRAMPA! Who leaves the TV on when he falls asleep at night so that when I sneak out of bed at night I can watch it? GRAMPA! He's the coolest growed-up, and we gotta find his teeth!"

**Grandpa doesn't approve of:** The way Stu and Didi are bringing up Tommy. He was brought up the old-fashioned way, and had to walk fifteen miles through the snow to get to school.

**He loves to tell Tommy:** Long stories about the old days, which always end with him fading off into a snoring nap

**Enjoys:** Fishing and bowling

**Calls Tommy:** Scout

**Refers to the Rugrats as:** Sprouts

**Stu calls Grandpa:** Pops

**Belongs to:** Old men's club called the "Royal Order of Wombats"

**Before he retired, Grandpa owned:** A repair shop

### A Grandpa moment:

"A puppet show for one-year-olds? What is this world coming to? Why, when I was a spud, we didn't have puppet shows. If we wanted entertainment, we went out to the back forty and pulled up stumps."

Grandpa has been played by two actors: **David Doyle** was Grandpa on the first sixty-five episodes and recorded several later episodes as well. The veteran actor died in 1997 at age sixty-seven. He was best known for playing Bosley, the boss of the three female private detectives on the 1970s hit *Charlie's Angels.*

Doyle was replaced by **Joe Alaskey**, who has much experience in the cartoon field portraying Bugs Bunny, Daffy Duck, and other Looney Tunes characters in commercials.

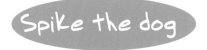

## Spike the dog

**Role:** Tommy's friend

**Character:** Friendly, loyal mutt whose main interest is food

**May not be able to talk, but:** Spike is often more aware of what the Rugrats are up to than their parents are.

**Likes to:** Take the Rugrats on his own adventures around the neighborhood

**Tommy likes to:** Ride Spike like a horse

**Hates:** Angelica's cat, Fluffy

**Comes to the rescue when:** Big, mean dogs want to attack Tommy

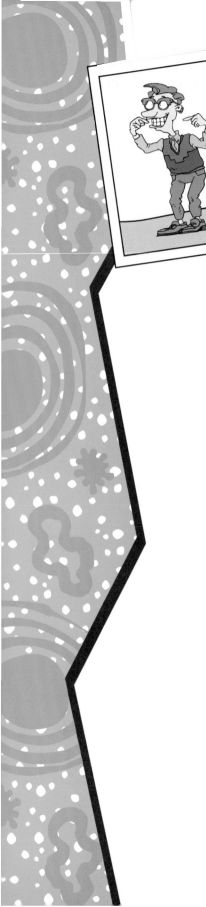

## Drew Pickles

**Role:** Stu's competition

**Character:** Stu's older brother, a rich banker. Unlike Stu, Drew always dresses neatly. Drew is Angelica's father.

**Personality:** Normal. Cares mostly about money and making Angelica happy

**When they were kids:** Stu and Drew fought all the time.

**Now that they're adults:** Stu and Drew still fight, but not as much.

**Fights always broken up by:** Grandpa

**Has no idea that:** Angelica is the biggest bully around.

**Discipline:** Rarely believes in it

**His car license plate says:** DREW

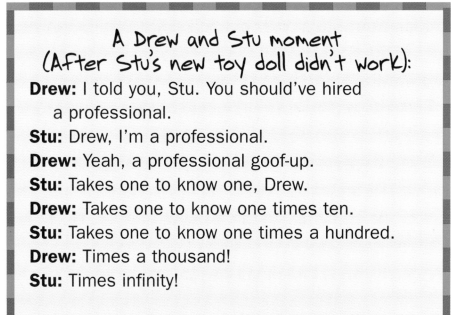

A Drew and Stu moment
(After Stu's new toy doll didn't work):

**Drew:** I told you, Stu. You should've hired
  a professional.
**Stu:** Drew, I'm a professional.
**Drew:** Yeah, a professional goof-up.
**Stu:** Takes one to know one, Drew.
**Drew:** Takes one to know one times ten.
**Stu:** Takes one to know one times a hundred.
**Drew:** Times a thousand!
**Stu:** Times infinity!

Drew is played by:
**Michael Bell**
He also does the voice of Grandpa Boris and
Chuckie's dad. Bell has worked on more than two
hundred cartoons besides *Rugrats,* including
*Superfriends, G. I. Joe,* and *Opus.*

## Charlotte Pickles

**Role:** The opposite of Didi

**Character:** Drew's wife, Tommy's aunt, mother of Angelica

**Personality:** More interested in her career than her family

**Best known for:** Always having a cellular phone attached to her ear

**Reason:** A very successful businesswoman, Charlotte is usually about to make a big new business deal. She's one of the top bosses at the MergeCorp company.

**Line:** "Something I learned in life, and that's to be a self-starter. Everything I am today, I have done myself."

**Assistant's name:** Jonathan

**Have you ever noticed:** Charlotte's mouth is on either her left or right side when she talks—but never in the middle!

**Spoils Angelica:** Even more than Drew

### A Charlotte Moment:

"I mean, Angelica just has it. Showbiz is in her blood. I had it. My father had it. And my great-uncle thought he had it, but it turned out to be poison ivy."

Charlotte is played by:
**Tress MacNeille**
Besides Charlotte, she plays Grandma on Nickelodeon's *Hey Arnold!* She is also a frequent voice on *The Simpsons,* where she plays the characters of Jimbo Jones and Lisa's friend Janey, as well as many guest voices in the mythical city of Springfield, USA.

## Charles Finster, Sr.

**Role:** Single dad

**Nickname:** Chaz

**Character:** Charles Finster Sr. is Chuckie's dad. Single, he has to act as mommy and daddy for Chuckie.

**Personality:** Well-meaning, hardworking dad.

**Line:** "When I was a kid, Christmas was always kind of disappointing. The best gift I ever got was a rubber glove and a tongue depressor."

**Shares in common with Didi:** A love of child-care expert Dr. Lipschitz

**Looks:** Just like Chuckie, just older, and with a mustache

**Listens to:** Latvian folk dance music

**Doesn't like sports:** Chaz would rather watch the chess championships than the football Ultra Bowl.

## A "Chaz" moment:

"What if Chuckie wakes up in the middle of the night and it's windy and the house is making all kinds of eerie noises? I might—I mean, he might be scared."

Charles Sr. is played by:
**Michael Bell**
He's also the voice of Grandpa Boris and Drew Pickles.

## Howard and Betty DeVille

### Betty

**Role:** Didi's sidekick

**Character:** Phil and Lil's mom and Didi's best friend. She lives next door and is a handy-woman who likes to fix things. Betty is also a health nut who loves to run in marathons.

**Personality:** Big, loud, and friendly woman

**Line:** "How the heck are you?"

**Best known for:** Talking like a man and always wearing sweatpants

**Often:** Baby-sits for the Rugrats

**Likes to drink:** Fancy coffee. Plenty of it. All the time.

**Has been seen:** Giving a friendly-but-painful backslap to Didi

**Prefers to:** Have the twins locked up behind baby gates and playpens so she can have peaceful moments alone

### Howard

**Role:** Guy to test new inventions for Stu

**Character:** Stu and Didi's next-door neighbor; Phil and Lil's dad

**Personality:** Small, shy, and quiet; never gets a word in around his loud wife

**Line:** "Well, Betty—"

**Good friends with:** Chuckie's dad

**Once got into a big fight with:** Stu—over a game of charades

> ## A Howard and Betty moment:
> **Betty:** We're totally psyched for this party thing. Aren't we, Howard?
> **Howard:** Well, Betty—
> **Betty:** Oh, don't mind Howard. He's just a little fazed on account of all these kids.
> **Howard:** Actually—
> **Betty:** I mean, the twins are enough of an armload. Say, do you think we could just pen these pups?

Betty DeVille is played by:
**Kath Soucie**
She also does the voices for Phil and Lil.

Howard DeVille is played by:
**Phil Proctor**
He was a member of the 1970s comedy group, The Firesign Theater.

## Boris and Minka

**Role:** Didi's parents

**Character:** Tommy's grandparents from "the old country." They live near Stu and Didi.

**So where is the old country?** Russia

**Best known for:** Arguing. They usually start in English and then end up in their original language, which no one else understands.

**While arguing:** Everyone else usually ignores them.

**Minka's specialty:** The Russian dish of borscht (beet soup)

### A Boris and Minka moment:

**Boris:** Vhat kind of cake is this? It should have been chocolate. In de old country, you never have carrot cake at a birthday party.

**Minka:** This isn't the old country, or haven't you noticed, Mr. Chocolate Cake?

**Boris:** For your information, chocolate cake is international.

**Minka:** Suddenly he's Mr. International.

Boris and Minka are played by:
**Melanie Chartoff and Michael Bell**
She also does Didi, and he does Drew and Chaz.

**Role:** The wise older kid (she's three) and Angelica's foil

**Character:** Tommy and the babies look up to their friend Susie; she's always around to help them out when they need the wisdom of an older kid.

**Personality:** Susie stands up for what's right—which often puts her right in Angelica's way.

**Line:** "Of course babies work. It's called 'playing!'"

**Best known for:** Her over-achieving mom and her famous dad—the creator of the *Dummi Bears* cartoon

**Often:** Shares her sandbox with the Rugrats

### A Susie moment:

**Tommy:** Hey, Susie, howcum you're wearing the same clothes as Cynthia?

**Susie:** 'Cause I was just at ballet class

**Chuckie:** What's that?

**Susie:** It's kinda like school, 'cept in ballet class we dance to music

Susie Carmichaels is played by:

## Cree Summer

Cree is best known for her role on the TV show, *A Different World*. She's also been doing cartoon voices since she was twelve years old, on shows such as *Tiny Toons Adventures, Sonic the Hedgehog, Ghostbusters, Pepper Ann,* and *Jungle Cubs.*

# Chapter Three

## THE MAKING OF "RUGRATS"

**C**an you believe that every half hour (actually twenty-two minutes, excluding commercials) of *Rugrats* takes ten months to make? It's true. And before the program appears on your TV, more than one hundred people—writers, actors, artists, editors, musicians, and others—have worked together to make it. It takes hours and hours—along with thousands of drawings—to make still pictures look like they can actually move. Artists have to draw more than ten thousand drawings to make just one eleven-minute *Rugrats* cartoon.

Animated cartoons have been around for more than eighty years. Most people think Walt Disney's *Mickey Mouse* was the first animated cartoon character. That's not true. *Felix the Cat, Oswald the Rabbit*, and *Gertie the Dinosaur* came before Mickey, but the black-and-white mouse in shorts was cartoon's first superstar.

When cartoons first started, they were silent and seen in movie theaters. Walt Disney is the guy who invented Mickey Mouse. He also made the first popular cartoon with sound, *Steamboat Willie,* in 1932, starring Mickey Mouse, of course. Disney also made the first full-length animated movie, *Snow White and the Seven Dwarfs,* in 1937.

Many of the cartoon characters that your grandparents grew up watching, like Mickey, Donald Duck, Popeye, Bugs Bunny, and Porky Pig, are still popular today because great cartoons never grow old. What was funny in 1937 is just as funny in 1997.

And speaking of great cartoons, this chapter shows step-by-step how a *Rugrats* cartoon goes from the writers' imaginations to your TV.

## 1. Writing

Some of the Rugrats Writers

Every *Rugrats* cartoon begins with words! Before any pictures can be drawn, everyone working on the show has to know what the episode will be about. That job goes to the writers. They come up with a story and gags (jokes) to keep you interested for eleven minutes. It's up to a team of writers to write the two eleven-minute *Rugrats* cartoons that appear in every episode. On the first sixty-five *Rugrats* shows, nine writers came up with the stories for Tommy, Chuckie, and the gang. One of them was Paul Germain, who helped create the show with Arlene Klasky and Gabor Csupo. After working on *Rugrats*, he made a new cartoon for Disney and ABC, called *Recess*. Craig Bartlett was another of the first writers. Later on, he created Nickelodeon's *Hey, Arnold!*

## 2. Acting

E. G. Daily & Christine Cavanaugh in recording studio

Once the script is complete, the actors come to Klasky Csupo's sound studios in Hollywood to record the characters' voices. Voice actors don't have to memorize their lines like other actors They just step in front of a microphone and read their lines from a script. They make funny faces and voices. And believe it or not, they get paid to do this! (The actors do get to read the scripts ahead of time so they will know what the story is about. This also gives them time to practice.)

Most young boy characters are voiced by women because a boy's voice changes when he becomes a teenager. Since cartoon characters rarely grow up—Tommy is always one year old and Chuckie is always two—cartoon voices have to stay the same. Two of the few cartoons to actually use kids' voices are *Hey, Arnold!* and the Charlie Brown TV specials.

## 3. Listening

The creative producer is the top boss. He or she is responsible for the sound and the look of the cartoon. After the actors record their voices, it is his or her job to listen to the story on tape. The actors usually read their lines several times, in different ways. After listening, the creative producer chooses the best one. Then a new copy of the tape is made for the director.

## 4. Directing

The director is in charge of how the cartoon looks on TV, just like the director of a movie. After he or she listens to the audio recording of the actors, the director decides who or what should be seen on the cartoon, at what angle, and for how long. The director also decides how the characters should act. For instance, if the script says for Angelica to

Creative producers

Animation director

yell at Tommy, what does Tommy look like while Angelica is yelling? The director makes these decisions and then instructs the storyboard artists (more on them in a minute) how he or she would like them to tell the story in drawings.

## 5. Designing Characters and Background

Someone has to decide what things should look like in a cartoon. That person is called a designer. There are three different kinds of designers who work on *Rugrats*—the character designer, the prop designer, and the background designer.

The *character designer* decides what new characters look like. If the Rugrats visit a movie theater and meet the guy who tears tickets in half, the character designer's job is to think of how the ticket-taker should look and then draw him or her.

The *background designer* draws the places where things happen. The Pickleses' living room looks the same in almost every show. But if they've never visited the movie theater before, the designer has to decide how it should look.

The *prop designer* draws things that the Rugrats come into contact with, like a big ball at the movie theater or a new toy that Stu Pickles invents.

## 6. Storyboarding

Storyboards are a series of pencil drawings that resemble frames in comic books. Each page of a storyboard contains three drawings that show a condensed version of the story. This helps the director show the animators

Prop designer

what the cartoon should look like when it's finished. Most eleven-minute *Rugrats* cartoons require storyboards of 250 to 300 pages. Since most storyboard artists draw about ten storyboard pages a day, Klasky Csupo needs a lot of them. It's more work than any one person could handle.

## 7. First Viewing

After the storyboards are drawn, they are run through a computer scanner. The tape of the actors' voices is also put into the computer, and a new tape is made, called the *animatic.* (The animatic sort of looks like one of those cartoon books you flip that makes it look like the characters are moving.) It gives the directors and producers an idea of what the cartoon will look like when it's done. From watching the animatic synchronized with the actors' voices, the director and producer can see if they need to fix any problems. Is the story too long or too short? How good do the storyboard pictures look? Are the characters moving the right way? These are the sorts of decisions the producers and director have to make.

## 8. Timing

Now the movements of the characters are timed. For instance, if Tommy crawls across the living room, how long will it take him to get there? That's important, because each cartoon is eleven minutes, not twelve or ten. The timing has to be perfect.

Storyboard artist

Animatic

## 9. The Lip Guy

This person is called "the Lip Guy" because his or her job is to listen to the cassette tape of the actors' voices and figure out how to make the characters' lips move. From years of experience of working on cartoons, "the Lip Guy" knows which mouth shapes will work with certain sounds. There is a list of mouth shapes ("A mouth," "B mouth," etc.) and he or she writes them down on a big sheet of paper next to the dialog from the script.

Checking supervisor-
Zsuzsa Lamy

## 10. Checking

You know how you check your homework before you hand it in? The same thing happens in 'toon land. Before the animation begins, all the storyboards, character and background designs, and other things have to be checked to make sure they're correct.

Color department artist

## 11. Coloring

Now more artists go to work. The job of the color department at Klasky Csupo is to decide how the animation should be colored. They use computers to help them. One main reason they do this is to make sure the colors of Chuckie, Tommy, and the others do not blend into the background. For instance, if they color a movie-theater lobby red, can Chuckie's red hair still be seen? Or should the theater lobby be colored green instead? If there are new characters or backgrounds needed, or new costumes for the babies, the color department works on them. Tommy, Chuckie, Angelica, Phil, and Lil are usually wearing the same clothes, but sometimes they have dreams of themselves as pirates or in some other fantasy situation and are dressed accordingly.

## 12. Drawing

Big boxes of storyboards, character drawings, backgrounds, and other stuff are sent from Klasky Csupo to the Anivision animation studio in Seoul, Korea, thousands of miles from Hollywood. This is where the final drawings for each episode are made. It takes more than ten thousand drawings to create an animated cartoon. First the Anivision artists draw the pictures on paper. These are then copied onto clear plastic sheets known as *cels*. The *Rugrats* animation is drawn in Korea because it would be too expensive to produce in the United States. Almost all TV cartoon animation is done in Asia now.

How do the animators in Korea know how to draw the characters? The character designers send them a "style guide," which contains many stock pictures of Tommy, Chuckie, Angelica, Phil, Lil, and their families, with specific facial expressions and poses. The style guide shows the animators how the characters look from the side, from behind, and from the front, as well as from other angles.

Top: Animation cel
Bottom: Design tips

## 13. Filming

After the artwork is done in Korea, the animation cels are photographed, one by one, using a special animation camera for cartoon production.

Animation has many little tricks to make the drawings look like real life. One such trick happens when the characters are walking. On TV it appears as if they are walking across the screen, but usually they are not. In fact, they are walking in place. What's really happening is that the characters are painted on clear cels and placed over the drawing of the background. When the cels are photographed, the background is moved behind them from one side of the screen to the other. That makes it look as if the characters are walking across the screen.

After the film is developed, it's sent back to Klasky Csupo in Hollywood.

## 14. Retakes

The producers and director watch the *rough cut* of the cartoon at Klasky Csupo to check for mistakes—for example, to see if any of the colors of the characters don't match (say Chuckie's hair is red in the beginning and orange by the end). If there is a problem, Klasky Csupo has the artists in Korea fix the drawings. Then they reshoot them and send back the corrected film.

## 15. Mixing and Editing

Next the picture editor combines the corrected film with the audiotape and puts the show into one piece. Since most *Rugrats* cartoons are eleven minutes long, sometimes he or she has to cut out some scenes or make them longer or shorter. Then the video is sent to the sound

Rerecording engineer Kurt Vanzo

department. There, *sound editors* watch the *Rugrats* video on TV monitors and decide which movements need sound to go with them. For instance, if you see a dog barking or a door slamming on screen, you need to hear those sounds, too. That's what the *sound mixer* does. Then the sounds are mixed with the actors' voices and the picture. This is done on a very expensive, powerful computer.

## 16. Composing the Music

The *music composer* now watches the tape and sits at the keyboard to invent music that will play in the background. You've probably never noticed, but most *Rugrats* cartoons have almost eight minutes of background music. The music is composed by Mark Mothersbaugh, formerly of the rock group Devo, and his partner and brother, Bob Mothersbaugh.

## 17. Completing

Now the cartoon is finally finished! Editors make three copies of the show and send them out to Nickelodeon's offices in New York, Los Angeles, and Orlando, Florida. Nickelodeon's main office is in New York. That's where all the shows are played from (more on that process in a minute). Nickelodeon's studios in Florida keep a copy of every Nick show in a permanent library, and a tape goes to Nick's LA offices, because that's where the animation division is, and they like to see the new 'toons!

Final videotape is ready to be sent to Nickelodeon

Klasky Csupo also sends a script of the episode to Nickelodeon's New York office because Nickelodeon shows are also played in other countries. *Rugrats* needs to be dubbed into other languages by other actors, so kids in France, Germany, and other places can understand what Chuckie and Tommy are saying. TV stations in other countries translate the English scripts into their language.

## 18. TV Time!

Ten months after the writers have handed in their script, Nickelodeon has a twenty-two-minute *Rugrats* episode from its TV network operations center in New York City. The Nick operations room has hundreds of VCRs playing all of the Nick shows, as well as the commercials.

The people who work there load all of the day's shows into the VCRs, and those TV pictures get sent electronically hundreds of thousands of miles into the sky to a huge satellite that flies in outer space. Cable TV systems receive the satellite signals and send the video and audio signals through a cable wire that goes to homes in their area.

And that's how *Rugrats* go from Los Angeles to Korea, to Los Angeles again, to New York, then to outer space and finally to your house!

# EPISODE GUIDE

**H**ere is a complete list of every *Rugrats* cartoon aired through the end of 1998. "A" stands for the first story of the *Rugrats* half hour; "B" is for the second one. After a two-year hiatus, many more episodes were created, as well as a full-length movie.

**1: "Tommy's First Birthday."** During Tommy's first birthday party, he and his friends decide that eating dog food will turn them into dogs. (This was a full twenty-two-minute episode.)

**2A: "Bar-B-Q."** Cousin Angelica hits Tommy's favorite ball over the fence during a Fourth of July picnic. Tommy and the other Rugrats journey into the neighbor's yard to retrieve it, where a huge watchdog scares them. Spike saves the day.

**2B: "Waiter, There's a Baby in My Soup."** Stu and Didi take Tommy to an important dinner for Dad's work, and Tommy makes a mess of the fancy restaurant.

**3A: "At the Movies."** The kids go to see their first film—starring the Dummi Bears. They get bored and crawl around the theater, where they destroy the popcorn counter and untangle film from eight different movies.

**3B: "Slumber Party."** Tommy dreams that his family has become the figures on the mobile that hangs over his crib.

**4A: "Baby Commercial."** Phil and Lil star in a TV diaper commercial.

**4B: "Little Dude."** Didi brings Tommy to the school where she teaches. Tommy gets lost on campus, ends up in a cafeteria food fight, and makes friends with the coolest guy at school.

**5A: "Beauty Contest."** When they discover a great fishing boat is the first prize in the "Little Miss Lovely" baby contest, Grandpa and Stu put a wig on Tommy and enter him in the pageant.

**5B: "Tommy at Bat."** Stu and Grandpa take Tommy to a baseball game, where he wanders around the stadium and takes part in the game.

**6A: "Ruthless Tommy."** Two bad guys mistake Tommy for a rich kid and kidnap him. They soon regret their crime when Tommy makes a mess out of their hangout.

**6B: "Moose Country."** The Rugrats hunt for wild moose in Tommy's backyard.

**7A: "Grandpa's Teeth."** Grandpa is supposed to play his trumpet at a big picnic, but Spike runs off with his false teeth.

**7B: "Momma Trauma."** Didi and Stu take Tommy to a baby psychologist after he crayons on the wall.

**8A: "Real or Robots."** Tommy wonders if his own father is a robot.

**8B: "Special Delivery."** Tommy climbs in the mailman's bag and ends up at the post office, where he's mistaken for a piece of mail and sent through the production line.

**9A: "Candy Bar Creep Show."** Stu and Didi build a haunted house for Halloween and the Rugrats sneak in, looking for Reptar bars. When they get tangled up in the props, Grandpa thinks the place is truly haunted.

**9B: "Monster in the Garage."** The adults blame Spike for a crash in the garage, but Tommy and the other babies are sure a monster did it. The babies head into the garage to meet him.

**10A: "Weaning Tommy."** Didi decides it's time for Tommy to stop using a bottle, but he doesn't want to let go of it.

**10B: "Incident in Aisle 7."** While grocery shopping with Grandpa, Tommy turns the store upside down in his search for Reptar cereal.

**11A: "Touch-Down Tommy."** Angelica decides she wants Tommy's chocolate milk bottle. Her attempt to steal the bottle— and Tommy's attempt to keep it—looks just like a football game.

**11B: "The Trial."** Who stole Tommy's clown lamp? That's what the Rugrats want to find out.

**12A: "Fluffy vs. Spike."** Angelica brings her cat Fluffy over to the Pickleses' house, and to Spike, Fluffy seems like Angelica's evil twin.

**12B: "Reptar's Revenge."** At the Sleazola Bros. Carnival, a guy in a rubber Reptar suit is giving out samples of Reptar cereal. Angelica runs off with his bag and everyone follows her on a wild chase that ends in the Tunnel of Love.

**13A: "Graham Canyon."** Stu and Didi take Tommy and Angelica on vacation, but their car breaks down. The Rugrats have a wild adventure in the auto repair shop.

**13B: "Stu Maker's Elves."** Tommy and Chuckie toss their glider plane into the basement, where they explore Stu's workshop and fix one of his creations.

**14A: "Toy Palace."** By mistake, Tommy and Chuckie get left behind in a huge toy store after closing time.

**14B: "Sand Ho!"** The Rugrats imagine that they're buccaneers on the high seas after Grandpa reads them a pirate story. They battle the evil Admiral Angelica, who threatens to steal their hard-earned treasure chest.

**15A: "Chuckie versus the Potty."** When Chuckie spends a weekend at the Pickleses' house, Stu and Didi help him overcome his fear of the potty.

**15B: "Together at Last."** When Phil and Lil get in a fight over a toy, Tommy and Chuckie help the twins make up.

**16A: "The Big House."** Tommy gets put in a day-care center that he compares to a stay in prison.

**16B: "The Shot."** When Tommy has to go to the doctor to get a "rooster shot," he and another baby try to make an escape.

**17A: "Showdown at Teeter-Totter Gulch."** Tommy and Chuckie go to a new playground where the kids live in fear of a bully called "the junk-food kid."

**17B: "Mirrorland."** Didi brings home a strange mirror. Tommy and Chuckie decide there is a reverse "Mirrorland" on the other side and imagine they enter it.

**18A: "Angelica's in Love."** Angelica gets a crush on a new four-year-old boy who wears a leather jacket and rides a big wheel.

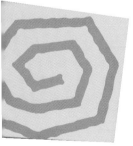

**18B: "Ice-Cream Mountain."** Bored with a game of miniature golf, the Rugrats wander off to find the great "Ice-Cream Mountain."

**19A: "Regarding Stuie."** When Stu is hit on the head and he can't remember who he is, he starts acting like a baby.

**19B: "Garage Sale."** The Pickles have a garage sale and the babies lend a hand by gathering up all of the adults' belongings. Only later do the adults realize the babies have sold all their things.

**20A: "Let There Be Light."** While Stu is testing a new electrical toy, the lights accidentally go out all over town. The babies decide "Mr. Light" is actually trapped in the refrigerator and they attempt to save him.

**20B: "The Bank Trick."** Tommy and Chuckie mistake the ATM machine for an M&M machine at the bank and search for its candy.

**21A: "Family Reunion."** On their way to a family gathering, Angelica tells Tommy that all parents give their kids away to other parents at family reunions. Scared out of his mind, Tommy recruits the help of all of his cousins at the reunion to remain with their parents.

**21B: "Grandpa's Date."** While baby-sitting Tommy and Chuckie, Grandpa is visited by an old love. Tommy and Chuckie try to help Grandpa have a good time with his girlfriend.

**22A: "No Bones About It."** At the Natural History Museum, Tommy and his pals see their first giant dinosaur skeleton and look for a souvenir bone for Spike.

**22B: "Beach Blanket Babies."** Chuckie's father buys him "sea monkeys"—tiny frozen shrimps— to keep as pets, but Chuckie believes the creatures will be happier in the ocean.

**23A: "Reptar on Ice."** The Rugrats find a little lizard and immediately assume that it must be Reptar's baby. Tommy takes it to an ice-skating show to reunite it with its mom.

**23B: "Family Feud."** The Rugrats set out to reunite the Pickleses and the DeVilles after they fight over a game of charades.

**24A: "Superhero Chuckie."** After watching TV's "Captain Blasto," the Rugrats convince Chuckie that he too can become a superhero when he puts on a purple cape.

**24B: "The Dog Broomer."** Didi hires a dog groomer to clean up Spike.

**25A: "Aunt Miriam."** After watching a science fiction movie about giant space ants, there's talk that Tommy's visiting Aunt Miriam might be such a creature.

**25B: "The Inside Story."** Inspired by a science-fiction movie, the Rugrats decide to shrink down with a "lazy beam" in order to get a watermelon seed out of Chuckie's tummy.

**26A: "A Visit from Lipschitz."** Didi meets her hero, famous child-care expert Dr. Lipschitz, at a bookstore and invites him over for dinner.

**26B: "What the Big People Do."** The Rugrats imagine what they would be like as adults.

**27: "The Santa Experience."** The families escape to a mountain cabin for the holidays. Things get a little out of hand when Tommy and Chuckie lay traps for Santa.

**28A: "Visitors from Outer Space."** Tommy dreams of being taken aboard an alien spaceship by aliens that look strangely like his parents.

**28B: "The Case of the Missing Rugrat."** Tommy is missing and Grandpa uses private detective skills to find him.

**29A: "Chuckie Loses His Glasses."** During a game of hide-and-go-seek, Chuckie loses his glasses. The whole world appears to him as a blurry nightmare.

**29B: "Chuckie Gets Skunked."** A skunk sprays Chuckie and it really bothers him—and everyone else.

**30A: "Rebel Without a Teddy Bear."** When Tommy's favorite stuffed animal gets taken away, he decides to take Angela's advice and become bad.

**30B: "Angelica the Magnificent."** Angelica gets a "Wee Wizard" magic kit as a gift, and the magical Angelica makes Lil disappear.

**31A: "Meet the Carmichaels."** Tommy becomes friends with his new neighbor, three-year-old Susie.

**31B: "The Box."** Stu buys Tommy a "Kiddie Karnival," but Tommy and his friends are more interested in the box it came in than what's inside.

**32A: "Down the Drain."** After Angelica tells them a horror story, Tommy and Chuckie develop a terrible fear of getting sucked down the bathtub drain.

**32B: "Let Them Eat Cake."** When Didi's younger brother Ben gets married, Tommy and Chuckie play with their uncle's big wedding cake.

**33A: "The Seven Voyages of Cynthia."** Tommy and Chuckie accidentally lose Angelica's favorite doll, Cynthia.

**33B: "My Friend Barney."** Chuckie says he has an imaginary friend, Barney, whom no one except Chuckie can see or hear.

**34A: "Feeding Hubert."** The Rugrats think the weekly garbage truck is really a monster named Hubert.

**34B: "Spike the Wonder Dog."** After the Rugrats see a TV show about a talking dog, they become convinced Spike can talk too.

**35A: "The Slide."** Susie and Tommy help Chuckie overcome his fear of slides.

**35B: "The Big Flush."** The babies go to a big swimming pool and mistake it for a giant potty. So where's the flusher?

**36A: "King Ten Pin."** The Rugrats fool around at a bowling alley when Grandpa competes in a senior bowling championship.

**36B: "Runaway Angelica."** Angelica decides to run away to Tommy's house when her dad punishes her.

**37A: "Game Show Didi."** Didi goes on a *Jeopardy!*-style game show.

**37B: "Toys in the Attic."** Boris and Minka take care of Tommy and Angelica for the weekend.

**38A: "Driving Miss Angelica."** Angelica saves Chuckie from getting hit by a troop of Big Wheel trucks, and she tells Chuckie he has to be her slave for life.

**38B: "Susie vs. Angelica."** Angelica challenges Susie to a contest to find out who the best kid on the block is.

**39A: "Tooth or Dare."** Angelica learns about the tooth fairy and forms a plan to get rich by pulling out Chuckie's teeth and putting them under her pillow.

**39B: "Party Animals."** Grandpa reads the Rugrats a story about Aladdin and his magic lamp, and they imagine what they would do with the wishes.

**40A: "Dummi Bear Dinner Disaster."** The producer of the *Dummi Bears* TV show comes over for dinner and the babies ruin the evening.

**40B: "Twins' Pique."** Sick and tired of their parents mixing up their names, Phil and Lil decide to act like different kids.

**41A: "Chuckie's First Haircut."** The Rugrats and Chaz try to help Chuckie overcome his fear of getting his first haircut.

**41B: "Cool Hand Angelica."** Angelica is sent to Susie's day camp, and she doesn't do well there.

**42A: "The Tricycle Thief."** Susie accuses Angelica of stealing her tricycle.

**42B: "Rhinoceritis."** Angelica plays doctor, telling Chuckie he has a disease that will turn him into a rhinoceros.

**43A: "Grandpa Moves Out."** Grandpa moves into a retirement home for old folks. Tommy and Angelica visit and convince him to move back home.

**43B: "The Legend of Satchmo."** Grandpa takes the Rugrats on their first camping trip—outside in the backyard. Stu, wandering around in the middle of the night to check on them, gets mistaken for the legendary "Satchmo" monster.

**44A: "Circus Angelicus."** Angelica stages her own circus, using the Rugrats as her three-ring acts.

**44B: "The Stork."** Angelica, when told that babies come from stork eggs, passes this on to the babies, who find a crow's egg and try to hatch a baby brother for Tommy.

**45A: "The Baby Vanishes."** Angelica puts "vanishing cream" on Tommy and Chuckie and pretends she can't see them in order to get them to sneak desserts for her.

**45B: "Farewell, My Friend."** Chuckie, deciding that Tommy plays too rough, stays away from his friend.

**46A: "When Wishes Come True."** Tommy wishes something bad would happen to Angelica after she's particularly nasty to him.

**46B: "Angelica Breaks a Leg."** Angelica, stuck at Tommy's house while her parents are on vacation, fakes a broken leg to get attention.

**47A: "The Last Baby-sitter."** Susie's teenage sister Alisa baby-sits Susie and Tommy for the first time, and the kids fear that monsters are loose in the house.

**47B: "Sour Pickles."** Grandpa tells Angelica and Tommy about what their parents were like as babies.

**48A: "Reptar 2010."** When the *Reptar 2010* video breaks, the Rugrats each supply their own ending to the story.

**48B: "Stu Gets a Job."** Having a problem coming up with new inventions, Stu goes out and gets a job. Tommy tries to keep his dad from leaving the house each morning.

**49A: "Give and Take."** After Chuckie admires Tommy's punching-bag clown doll, Tommy gives it to Chuckie. Tommy immediately misses the doll and asks Chuckie for it back.

**49B: "The Gold Rush."** The Rugrats find a nickel in the park. After that, they believe there's a gold mine of money in different parts of the playground.

**50A: "Home Movie."** As Stu shows boring pictures of his family's vacation, the Rugrats draw their own pictures about their lives.

**50B: "The Mysterious Mr. Friend."** Stu invents a talking, walking "Mr. Friend" doll, which seems to do strange things when alone with the babies.

**51A: "Cuffed."** Angelica gets stuck to Chuckie in a pair of toy handcuffs.

**51B: "The Blizzard."** Snow falls in the Rugrats' neighborhood, and the babies go off on a backyard fantasy adventure to find the North Pole; they need Santa to fix Chuckie's fire truck!

**52A: "Destination: Moon."** The babies mistake Grandpa's camping trailer for a rocket ship, then believe that they've blasted off to the moon.

**52B: "Angelica's Birthday."** Scared of getting older and having more responsibilities, Angelica pretends she's a baby.

**53A: "Princess Angelica."** Angelica believes she's an actual princess.

**53B: "The Odd Couple."** When Tommy stays with Chuckie for a few days, their personal habits start to annoy each other.

**54A: "Naked Tommy."** Tommy decides he'd rather go naked like his dog Spike.

**54B: "Tommy and the Secret Club."** Angelica forms a secret club and makes the babies compete to become members.

**55A: "Under Chuckie's Bed."** When Chuckie gets a big boy's bed, Angelica tells him there's a monster underneath it.

**55B: "Chuckie Is Rich."** Chaz wins ten million dollars in the American Dunderhead Sweepstakes, and everybody's nice to Chuckie—even Angelica.

**56A: "Mommy's Little Assets."** Tommy and Angelica go to Charlotte's office for the day.

**56B: "Chuckie's Wonderful Life."** Unhappy, Chuckie gets a visit from his guardian angel, who shows him how he's touched everyone's lives and what would have happened had he never been born.

**57A: "In the Dreamtime."** Chuckie has some wild dreams one night, and the next day the Rugrats have a hard time convincing him he's not still dreaming.

**57B: "The Unfair Pair."** Tired of being left out at Phil and Lil's house, Angelica tries to become the favorite.

**58A: "Chuckie's Red Hair."** Chuckie's sick of all the fuss people make over his red hair, so he gets Tommy to dye it black with Grandpa's dye.

**58B: "Spike Runs Away."** Spike runs away and Stu tries to replace him with a series of new pets for Tommy.

**59A: "The Alien."** Is Chuckie really an alien? Is his playhouse a rocket ship? That's what Angelica says.

**59B: "Mr. Clean."** Chuckie gets worried about germs and refuses to touch anything for fear of accidentally coming into contact with them.

**60A: "Angelica's Worst Nightmare."** Angelica's mom says she's pregnant, and Angelica worries that she'll be forgotten once the new baby arrives.

**60B: "The Mega Diaper Babies."** The Rugrats imagine they're super-heroes like TV's Mega Hyper Heroes. When the wicked Angelitron steals their Mega Hyper dolls, the Mega Diaper Babies are called to action.

**61A: "New Kid in Town."** Tired of Angelica's bullying, the Rugrats go play with another kid in the park, Josh.

**61B: "Pickles vs. Pickles."** Angelica decides to sue her parents after they make her eat broccoli.

**62: "Rugrats Passover."** A half-hour special in which the Rugrats go to Boris and Minka's for the Jewish holiday of Passover. They get locked

in the attic with Boris, who recounts the Passover story using the babies as historical characters.

**63A: "Kid TV."** The TV breaks, and the Rugrats use a cardboard box to create their own shows.

**63B: "The Sky Is Falling."** Chuckie believes the sky is falling and the babies take shelter to prepare for the coming disaster.

**64A: "I Remember Melville."** Chuckie adopts a pet, Melville the Bug. When the bug dies, Chuckie has a hard time accepting that Melville is no longer alive.

**64B: "No More Cookies."** After Angelica eats too many cookies and gets a stomachache, she makes the babies promise to keep the cookies away from her.

**65A: "Cradle Attraction."** Chuckie gets a crush on a new girl, Megan.

**65B: "Angelica's Moving Away."** At first the babies are glad to hear that Angelica's moving away. Then Tommy thinks about how Angelica's meanness helped them all unite against each other and become friends. Finally, Drew announces they're not moving after all, and the babies all cheer.

**Special Episode #999: "Rugrats Chanukah."** During a celebration at the synagogue, the babies try to help Boris overcome the Meany of Chanukah, who they believe is an old enemy of Boris's.

**Special Episode #998: "Rugrats Mother's Day."** The babies learn why they have never seen Chuckie's mom.

**Special Episode #997: "Rugrats Summer Vacation."** Stu and Didi take the babies to Las Vegas.

• • • • • • • • • • •

**Hiatus from production between May 1994 and June 1996**

• • • • • • • • • • •

**66A: "Spike's Babies."** Spike's behavior gets a little weird when he secretly adopts a litter of kittens that he has stashed under the house.

**66B: "Chicken Pops."** The Rugrats catch the chicken pox.

**67A: "Radio Daze."** The babies solve a mystery in a movie-like fantasy.

**67B: "Psycho Angelica."** Angelica convinces the babies that she can predict the future.

**68A: "America's Wackiest Home Movies."** Stu and Drew compete to win a prize on a TV video show, featuring videos of the babies.

**68B: "The 'Lympics."** The Rugrats try to save Angelica's gold necklace.

**69A: "Car Wash Monster."** The babies make a mess at the car wash.

**69B: "Heat Wave."** On a hot day at the playground, Tommy and his friends imagine they're in the desert.

**70A: "Angelica's Last Stand."** The babies help Angelica open a lemonade stand.

**70B: "Clan of the Duck."** Chuckie and Phil discover that dresses are "cooler" than pants.

**71A: "Faire Play."** After a story from Grandpa Lou, the Rugrats imagine themselves in fairy-tale land.

**71B: "Smell of Success."** Chuckie gets a better sense of smell.

**72: "The Turkey Who Came to Dinner."** The babies become friends with a turkey and try to save him from being eaten in this Thanksgiving Day special.

**73A: "Potty Training Spike."** Chuckie decides to teach Spike everything he is learning about switching from diapers to the potty.

**73B: "Art Fair."** Angelica takes credit for the babies' childish artwork.

**74A: "Send in the Clouds."** The babies believe that Tommy's wish to be up in the clouds has come true when they see early morning fog outside.

**74B: "In the Navel."** The Rugrats go on their first boating trip.

**75A: "Mattress."** The Rugrats try to get the monster they believe is in Grandpa Lou's mattress out of their house.

**75B: "Looking for Jack."** On the way to a Dummi Bears concert, the minivan breaks down and the babies end up at an Italian restaurant instead.

**76A: "Hiccups."** Tommy gets the hiccups.

**76B: "Autumn Leaves."** When the leaves start to change colors, the babies think the trees are sick.

**77A: "Dust Bunnies."** During spring cleaning, Tommy and Chuckie think a dust bunny is an animal out to get them.

**77B: "Educating Angelica."** At show-and-tell day at school, Angelica presents Tommy.

**78A: "The Ransom of Cynthia."** Angelica tries to steal candy from the babies.

**78B: "Turtle Recall."** The babies lose their dads in a department store and focus on reuniting a turtle with its dad.

**79A: "Angelica Orders Out."** Angelica gets a hold of Stu's new invention and uses it to change her voice.

**79B: "Let It Snow."** The babies think it's Christmas in August after they pose for their Christmas card.

**80A: "Angelica Nose Best."** After she wakes up with a swollen nose, Angelica thinks she's Pinocchio and vows to turn over a new leaf.

**80B: "Pirate Light."** The babies believe a repairman is actually a pirate.

**81A: "Grandpa's Bad Bug."** After Grandpa Lou announces that he caught a "bad bug," the babies think he ate an insect and try to cure him.

**81B: "Lady Luck."** Grandpa brings the Rugrats to play bingo.

**82A: "Crime and Punishment."** Chaz gets a crush on a female traffic cop.

**82B: "Baby Maybe."** Stu and Didi's friends Ben and Elaine are thinking about having a baby and baby-sit for one night as a test run.

**83A: "The Word of the Day."** Angelica tries out to be the new junior assistant for "Miss Carol's Happy House."

**83B: "Jonathan Baby-sits."** Charlotte forces her assistant Jonathan to baby-sit.

**84A: "He Saw, She Saw."** Chuckie becomes friends at the park with Emma, sister of Big Binky, an over-protective three-year-old.

**84B: "Piggy's Pizza Palace."** The Rugrats make a mess at the local pizzeria/video arcade.

**85A: "Fugitive Tommy."** Tommy is mistaken for a one-toothed baby who has gotten into trouble.

**85B: "Visiting Aunt Miriam."** When one of Grandpa Lou's lady-friends says that Chuckie looks "good enough to eat" the babies naturally worry that Chuckie is about to be eaten.

**86A: "The First Cut."** Tommy is rattled when he gets his first cut.

**86B: "Chuckie Grows."** The babies think Chuckie is growing after Grandpa Lou accidentally shrinks his clothes in the wash.

**87A: "Uneasy Rider."** Angelica takes Chuckie under her wing when he gets his first bike.

**87B: "Where's Grandpa?"** During a trip, Grandpa Lou gets stranded at a gas station, and the Rugrats work hard to reunite with him.

**88A: "The Wild, Wild West."** The Rugrats imagine they're cowboys in the Old West.

**88B: "Angelica For a Day."** After Angelica explains the expression "to be in the other guy's shoes," Tommy decides to make Chuckie braver by putting him in Angelica's shoes.

**89A: "Baby-Sitting Fluffy."** Chaz and Chuckie are forced to baby-sit Angelica's nasty pet cat Fluffy when Angelica and her family leave town.

**89B: "Sleep Trouble."** During a sleepover, Tommy and Chuckie fear that the Sandman is coming to get them, and they set elaborate traps for him.

**90A: "Journey to the Center of the Basement."** The babies make a trek to the basement in order to save Chuckie's favorite Reptar Jr. toy.

**90B: "A Very McNulty Birthday."** When the Rugrats go to a birthday party at the McNulty's house, they are set against one another when Timmy McNulty tells the girls they can't play because they have cooties.

**91: "The Family Tree."** In the episode that leads to *Rugrats: The Movie*, Tommy and Chuckie discuss other members of their family, and at the end, learn that Didi is pregnant again.

Feature film, *Rugrats: The Movie*

## The End

Congratulations—you're now a Rugrats expert!

If there's more you want to know, write to me in care of Simon & Schuster. You can also e-mail me at JeffersonGraham@prodigy.net.

## About the Author

Jefferson Graham is the author or coauthor of nine nonfiction books on subjects such as Las Vegas, TV game shows, and the *Frasier* TV show. A staff writer for *USA Today* since 1984, he has written about many different things, including television, pizza, ice cream, roller coasters, cartoons, and pancakes. As a photographer, he specializes in taking pictures of milk shakes, cows, and his son Sam on water slides. He lives in Los Angeles, California.